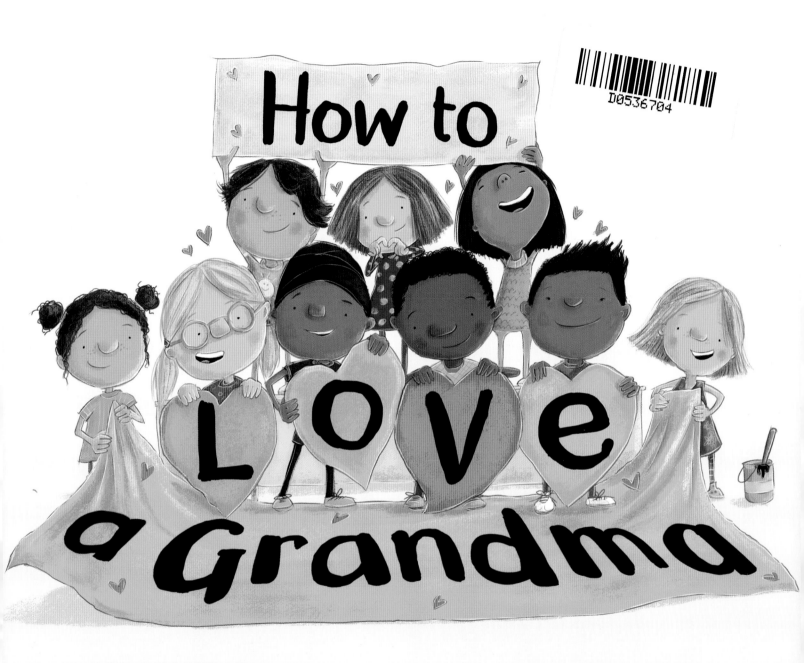

How to Love a Grandma

BY JEAN REAGAN ♥ ILLUSTRATED BY LEE WILDISH

ALFRED A. KNOPF ⚘ NEW YORK

You love your grandma—
SOOOOOO much!
A snuggly way to show her is to . . .

. . . HUG her!

Try a . . .

. . . look-how-tall-I've-grown hug.

Make-it-all-better hug.

Or faraway air hug.

Grandma also feels loved when you **SHARE** with her . . .

. . . a ladybug, from your finger to hers.

A seat on a crowded bus.

The biggest strawberry.

Your secret reading nest.

Love your grandma by keeping her **SAFE**.

Push the "walk" button
before you cross the street.

Say, "Seat belts!" as you get in the car.

Hand her your favorite oven mitt.

Remind her to ask before petting someone's dog.

Love your grandma? **HELP** your grandma!

Fill the bird feeder.

Find the penguins at the zoo.

Pull the sled up the hill.

Reach things under her bed.

Sometimes, you can love Grandma by helping her feel **BRAVE**.

Hold her hand for big waves.

Walk fast past the lions together.

Whisper, "Ready? Set? Now!"
as you step onto an escalator.

When thunder crashes,
let her hold your teddy bear.

If you want your grandma to feel extra loved, **CHEER** for her.
Say, **"Yay, Grandma!"** when she . . .

. . . learns your tricky move.

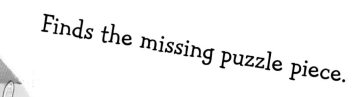

Finds the missing puzzle piece.

Figures out your car seat.

Takes a bow.

You LOVE Grandma, and Grandma LOVES you.
Can you tell each other at the exact *same* time?

Ready?

"One—two—three. I—LOVE—YOU!"
(Try it faster, *faster*, **faster!**)

Now, blow a kiss, and give your grandma one more

giant,

squeezy,

snuggly

I-love-you hug.